Maria
the Mother's Day
Fairy

Join the **Rainbow Magic Reading Challenge!**

Read the story and collect your fairy points to climb the
Reading Rainbow at the back of the book.

This book is worth 10 points.

For Abigail Brooks, with love x

Special thanks to
Rachel Elliot

ORCHARD BOOKS

First published in Great Britain in 2018 by The Watts Publishing Group

1 3 5 7 9 10 8 6 4 2

© 2018 Rainbow Magic Limited.
© 2018 HIT Entertainment Limited.
Illustrations © Orchard Books 2018

A CIP catalogue record for this book is available from the British Library.

ISBN 978 1 40834 965 6

Printed and bound in Great Britain by CPI Group (UK) Ltd, Croydon, CR0 4YY

MIX
Paper from
responsible sources
FSC® C104740

The paper and board used in this book are made from wood from responsible sources

Orchard Books
An imprint of Hachette Children's Group
Part of The Watts Publishing Group Limited
Carmelite House, 50 Victoria Embankment, London EC4Y 0DZ

An Hachette UK Company
www.hachette.co.uk
www.hachettechildrens.co.uk

Maria
the Mother's Day
Fairy

by Daisy Meadows

ORCHARD

www.rainbowmagic.co.uk

The Fairyland Palace

Maria's Cottage →

← Tippington Youth Club

TIPPINGTON TOWN

Jack Frost's Spell

"I love my mum," the goblins squawk.
I can't abide their silly talk.
They spout such sentimental slop.
This mumsy nonsense has to stop!

Maria is the one to blame.
I'll take her things and bring her shame.
The goblin mums won't get a mention.
And I'll have everyone's attention!

The
Brilliant Bracelet

Contents

Chapter One: Mother's Day Plans   11

Chapter Two: News From Fairyland   25

Chapter Three: A Country Cottage   37

Chapter Four: Goblin Cleaners   45

Chapter Five: Flattering Frost   53

Mother's Day Plans

"Are you sure you don't mind being away from your mum tomorrow?" said Rachel Walker for the fifth time that morning. "After all, it is Mother's Day."

"I'm sure," said her best friend, Kirsty Tate. "I've left my card and present with Dad, and he promised to give them to

Mum first thing tomorrow morning.
Besides, I'll see her tomorrow evening
when I get home. I'm so happy to be
spending a whole weekend with you in
Tippington!"

She gave a little skip of excitement, and
Rachel flashed her a smile. Even though
she had lots of friends in Tippington,
there was no one as special as Kirsty.
They had been best friends almost
from the first moment they had met on
holiday on Rainspell Island. It had been
the most exciting holiday the girls had
ever known, because they had made
friends with the Rainbow Fairies and
helped them to defeat Jack Frost and his
naughty goblins. Since then, they had
shared many magical adventures with
their fairy friends.

"I wonder if we'll see any fairies this weekend," said Rachel.

"I hope so," said Kirsty, smiling. "Fingers crossed for lots of fairies and no goblins!"

Rachel and Kirsty had always kept their promise to Queen Titania that they would never tell anyone else about the fairies. They could only talk about magic with each other.

"I wish I had a magic spell to help me think of the perfect gift for Mum," Rachel went on.

It was Saturday morning, and the girls were on their way into town. Rachel wanted to pick out a special gift for her mum, but she was stuck for ideas.

"I'm sure you'll find the perfect thing in town," said Kirsty. "Oh, what's this?"

She stopped to read a poster taped to a lamppost.

Tippington Youth Club Needs YOU!
Do you want to do something extra special
for your mum this Mother's Day?
Pop along to the youth club on Saturday
morning to find out more.

"That sounds like just the sort of thing I need," said Rachel in delight. "How lucky that you spotted it."

"Let's go to the youth club right now and ask what they're planning," said Kirsty.

Rachel led the way to the church hall. The doors were wide open.

"They hold the youth club here every Saturday morning," said Rachel as they went in. "It's always lots of noisy fun."

"It's not very loud right now," said Kirsty.

There were lots of children in the hall, but they were all sitting around looking bored. One girl was throwing a ball against the wall and catching it. Another was colouring in a big sign that said 'Happy Mother's Day'. As the girls watched, she dropped her pen and let out a long sigh.

There was a long table in the middle of the hall, filled with presents that the children had bought for their mothers, as well as wrapping paper, ribbons and bows. But not a single child was wrapping up their present.

"There's Eliza," said Rachel. "She's the youth club leader. Oh dear, she looks worried. Let's go and find out what's wrong."

Rachel led Kirsty over to a young woman with long blonde hair.

"Hello, Eliza," she said. "We saw the poster about Mother's Day. I don't have a present for my mum yet and I'm hoping to get some ideas."

"Hi, Rachel," said Eliza. She tried to give them all a smile, but was looking sad. "I'm afraid that no one in the youth club seems very interested in Mother's Day right now," she sighed. "I've planned a surprise Mother's Day Picnic for tomorrow. I wanted to give everyone a chance to surprise their mums and show them how much they love them. The children were keen at first, but now they just seem grumpy about it."

A frown creased her forehead, and Rachel felt sorry for her.

"We'll help," she said at once. "Won't we, Kirsty?"

"Of course," said Kirsty, nodding. "What would you like us to do?"

"Could you try to get the others over to the card-making table?" Eliza asked.

"Every mother should have a beautiful
card on Mother's Day."

The card-making table was neatly
arranged with piles of yellow card, lacy
white doilies, sparkly jewel stickers,
scissors and glue.

"Come on, everyone," said Rachel, beckoning to the bored-looking children around the hall. "I've got a great idea for an easy card to make."

The other children gathered around and Rachel showed them how to cut out a yellow flower shape and stick it on to a doily. Slowly, they began to copy her design. But after a few minutes, more than half of them had wandered off. The others were making careless mistakes and wasting paper.

"They don't seem to want to do nice things for their mums," said Rachel to

Kirsty under her breath.

"I wonder why they bothered to come along at all," said Kirsty.

After a little while, Kirsty noticed that all the doilies had been used up. Several of them had been ripped, and others were lying on the floor.

"Let's get some more and make the cards ourselves," she suggested. "Perhaps the others will want to join in when they see how much fun we're having."

Eliza told them that there were more doilies in the supply bags.

"They're under the window at the back of the hall," she said.

As Rachel and Kirsty headed towards the bags, they noticed a vase of daffodils on the windowsill.

"Daffodils always make me think of Mother's Day," Rachel said with a smile.

The girls bent over the first bag and found the doilies. But when they stood up, Kirsty saw something strange.

"Rachel, look,"

she whispered. "One of the daffodils is glowing."

The girls exchanged a thrilled glance. That golden glow could mean only one thing.

Magic!

News from Fairyland

Rachel and Kirsty leaned forwards and peered at the glowing daffodil. They saw a tiny fairy sitting inside the trumpet-like part of the flower.

"Hello," whispered Kirsty, tingling with excitement. "Welcome to Tippington."

"Hello," said the fairy in a gentle voice. "I'm Maria the Mother's Day Fairy."

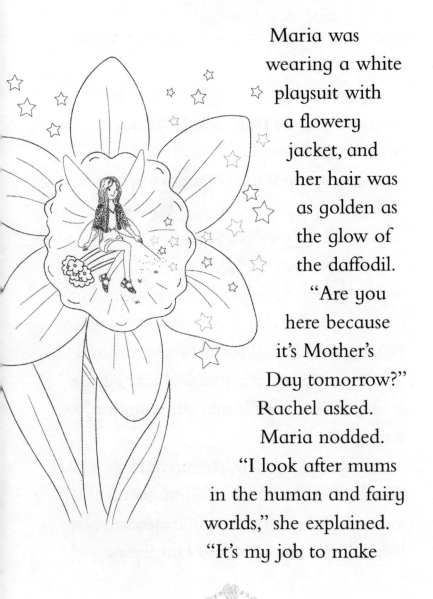

Maria was
wearing a white
playsuit with
a flowery
jacket, and
her hair was
as golden as
the glow of
the daffodil.
"Are you
here because
it's Mother's
Day tomorrow?"
Rachel asked.
Maria nodded.
"I look after mums
in the human and fairy
worlds," she explained.
"It's my job to make

sure they get on well with their sons and daughters."

"I think something might have gone wrong here," said Rachel, glancing over her shoulder. "No one seems very interested in making tomorrow special."

"It's not just here," said Maria with a worried frown. "Mother's Day events all over the human and fairy worlds are having problems, and I can't put things right by myself. I've come to ask for your help."

"Of course we'll help you," said Kirsty at once. "But why is everything going wrong?"

"Yesterday, we held a festival in Fairyland to celebrate the magic of mums," Maria explained. "Everyone was talking about mums, and we were delighted when lots of goblins turned up to join in the fun."

"Did they cause trouble?" Rachel guessed.

She was surprised when Maria shook her head.

"No, they were really well behaved," said the fairy. "They talked about their mums and made lots of little presents for them. It was lovely, but I hadn't realised how much it would annoy Jack Frost."

"I had almost forgotten that goblins have mums," said Rachel.

"Me too," said Kirsty. "But now I remember seeing them when we visited Goblin Grotto."

"Jack Frost never lets the goblin mums work for him in the castle," said Maria. "He can't make them do what he says,

and they always tell him that his revenge plans are silly and he should try counting to ten to control his temper."

The girls giggled at the thought of a group of goblin mums telling Jack Frost off. No wonder he didn't like mums!

"Why should he get cross about you celebrating the magic of mums?" asked Kirsty.

"Because he thought the goblins should

be waiting on him hand and foot, not
having fun at a festival," said Maria. "He
blamed me, so he got his revenge in the
most horrible way. He crept into my
cottage and stole my precious magical
objects."

"Oh no, that's awful," said Rachel,
wishing that she was small enough to
give Maria a hug.

"He also left a mean message on my
door," Maria went on. "It said that he is
fed up of silly mumsy
talk, and he's going
to stop everyone
talking about
mothers once
and for all."
She looked at
the girls and they

saw that tears were brimming in her eyes.

"The magic of motherhood is going all wonky, and I don't know what to do," she said. "Queen Titania said that if anyone could get my magical objects back, it would be you two. Will you come to Fairyland and help me to search for them?"

"Of course we will," said Rachel. "We can't let Jack Frost spoil Mother's Day."

Maria raised her wand.

"Ready?" she asked.

The girls glanced around. The other children had wandered away from the card-making table and no one was looking their way.

"Now," said Rachel and Kirsty together.

There was a rushing, whooshing sound, and then the daffodils in the vase seemed

to grow as tall as trees. Next moment, the girls realised that they were no longer standing on the hall floor. They were hovering beside the flowers on gossamer wings, as tiny as hummingbirds. The daffodils hadn't grown. The girls had shrunk!

Gasping with the suddenness of it, Rachel and Kirsty hugged in mid-air. Maria fluttered towards them, her cheeks dimply with smiles.

"Come on," she said. "Let's go before

anyone sees us."

She took their hands and flew towards
the daffodil where she had been sitting.
Landing in the
trumpet-like
centre, she sat
down with her
feet pointing
into the flower.

"Is this
the way to
Fairyland?"
asked Kirsty.

"It's one of

them," said Maria. "Follow me."

She slid into the centre of the flower as
if she were going down a slide. Instantly,
there was a flash of golden sparkles, and
Maria had disappeared.

"I can't wait to try this," said Rachel, sitting down.

Kirsty sat beside her, and they pushed off together. Golden sparkles flashed around them as they zoomed into the velvety yellow tube. A fresh springtime scent floated deliciously up and they whizzed downwards, holding hands and squealing in delight.

"This has to be the most amazing slide in the world," cried Kirsty. "Fairyland, here we come!"

A Country Cottage

Rachel and Kirsty shot out of the daffodil slide and landed on soft cushions with a bump.

"Best slide ever," said Rachel, grinning as she jumped up.

"I hope we get to do that again one day," said Kirsty, brushing daffodil pollen off her skirt.

They had landed in the middle of a country garden, full of colourful wildflowers and busy honey bees. A toadstool cottage had grown in the middle of the garden, and Maria was standing in front of it.

"Welcome to my home," she said, opening the door.

Rachel and Kirsty felt at home as soon as they walked inside. Maria's cottage was neat and bright, with flowers on every table and the scent of baking in the air.

"Oh, my mum's got that cushion on her special chair," said Rachel, pointing to a cushion embroidered with a unicorn.

Maria smiled as if she already knew.

"And that's my mum's favourite painting hanging on the wall," said Kirsty. "This is a lovely cottage. I hope that Jack Frost didn't make too much mess when he sneaked in."

Maria's smile faded.

"No," she said. "He only took my magical objects, which was bad enough."

"What are your magical objects?"
Rachel asked. "What do we need to look
for?"

"There are three things," said Maria.
"The first is the brilliant bracelet, which
helps children be kind to their mums and
want to do nice things for them. The
second is the handy handbag. It looks
after the gifts given to mothers by their
children. Lastly, the mummy mirror helps
me to remember all the mums I've ever
met, and how to help them."

Rachel and Kirsty exchanged worried
glances.

"Those are all really important things
every day," said Kirsty. "But they matter
even more on Mother's Day."

"Yes, and now Jack Frost has them,
mother magic is going wrong all over

Fairyland and the human world," said Maria.

"Is that why the children in the youth club were so thoughtless about Mother's

Day?" Rachel asked.

Maria nodded.

"The brilliant bracelet helps children be kind to their mums and want to do nice things for them," she said. "Without it, the

children have stopped caring about the
Mother's Day Picnic."

"We have to stop Jack Frost from
making things any worse," said Kirsty,
putting her hands on her hips. "Let's
start at Jack Frost's Ice Castle. He's
probably taken
everything
there so he
can boast
to the goblins
about how clever
he is."

"Then it's time for us to
stop him," said Maria.
She raised her wand,
and a flurry of
bright flower petals
whooshed around

them. When the petals vanished, they were standing on the edge of a snowy forest, gazing up at Jack Frost's castle.

Goblin Cleaners

"I've never seen Jack Frost's castle look so busy before," said Rachel in surprise.

Even from a distance, they could see that the castle was bustling with activity. There were goblins balancing on tall ladders, polishing windows and brushing down the stone walls. There were goblins sweeping the battlements and scrubbing the drawbridge. There were even goblins inside ironing the curtains – while they were still hanging up.

"I've never seen the goblins work so hard," said Kirsty.

"Or the castle look so clean," added Rachel. "I wonder what's going on."

"One thing's for certain," said Maria. "With so many goblins around, we won't be able to get in without being seen."

"We need a disguise," said Kirsty.

"I've got an idea," said Rachel. "Maria, can you turn us into goblin cleaners? We'd fit right in today."

Maria smiled and waved her wand. At once, their wings disappeared. Their skin turned green and lumpy, and their heads became completely bald. Instead of their normal clothes, they were each wearing a

stripy uniform labelled 'Green and Clean'.
Rachel had three mops, Maria held a
silver bucket, and Kirsty was carrying a
bag filled with dusters and polish.

"Let's go and get your magical objects
back," said Kirsty.

The disguised friends walked past
the goblins who were scrubbing the
drawbridge, and stopped to peer down at
more goblins who were polishing the ice
on the moat.

47

"You, cleaner goblins!" squawked an angry voice.

The goblin guard on the entrance was jabbing his finger at them.

"Stop gawping at the others and get inside the castle," he said. "There's work to be done. We have to get this place cleaned up."

"Why?" asked Rachel.

The goblin gaped at her.

"Why do you think, you nitwit?" he demanded. "It'll make Jack Frost happy." A dreamy look came over his face. "Jack Frost is like a mother to us, so we have to do everything we can to make him smile."

"A mother?" said Kirsty in amazement.

"Yes, of course," said Rachel quickly. "Come on, let's go and help clean up the Throne Room."

The guard goblin let them in, and they hurried to the Throne Room.

"What did that goblin mean?" Kirsty said in a whisper. "Jack Frost is nothing like a mother."

"He must have done something to make them think like that," said Rachel.

"It's because he's got my magical objects," Maria said with a sigh. "I'm

sure that they're only trying to make
him happy because he has the brilliant
bracelet."

They couldn't say any more because
they had reached the Throne Room.
The doors were wide open, and they
could see Jack Frost sitting on his throne,
surrounded by utter pandemonium.

Goblins were polishing the throne, cleaning the floor, ironing the curtains, wobbling on ladders to sweep the ceiling and dangling upside down to make the chandeliers sparkle. One goblin was even perching on the back of the throne, sewing up a hole in Jack Frost's cloak.

Maria squeezed Rachel's arm.

"I can see the brilliant bracelet," she whispered. "Oh, this is wonderful. We've found it!"

Rachel and Kirsty saw a golden bangle sparkling on Jack Frost's wrist. It was engraved with the word 'Mother'.

"Now we just have to find a way to get it back," said Rachel.

Flattering Frost

"Look at Jack Frost," said Kirsty.

The Ice Lord had been sitting very quiet and still. When the disguised fairies looked at his face, they guessed that he was only quiet because he was so angry.

"I am getting really, really sick of the smell of furniture polish," he hissed through gritted teeth. "I stole that silly fairy's things so that all the attention would be on me, not my castle."

"I've got an idea," said Rachel. "If we can get Jack Frost to let us clean the bracelet, he will have to take it off."

Maria's eyes sparkled and she slipped her hand inside her uniform to wave her wand. Instantly, the mops, bucket and bag disappeared. Rachel found herself holding a velvet pouch labelled 'Gold-cleaning kit'.

Kirsty stepped up to Jack Frost and tapped him on the shoulder.

"Excuse me, sir," she said in her squawky goblin voice. "May I just say that you look more handsome than ever today?"

"That's true," said Jack Frost.

"An important person like you should always look his best," said Maria. "But we were just thinking that your bracelet was looking a bit grubby."

"We're trained jewellery cleaners," said Rachel. "We can make your jewellery shine like never before. Please let us make you look your best."

She held out the velvet pouch. Jack Frost hesitated.

"Your jewellery should shine as splendidly as you do," said Kirsty.

Puffing out his chest, Jack Frost gave a self-satisfied smile.

"I *am* splendid," he said.

He removed the bracelet and placed it on the velvet pouch. At once, Rachel darted backwards.

"What are you doing?" cried Jack Frost.

"I'm returning this to its rightful owner," said Rachel.

She handed the bracelet
to Maria, who pulled
out her wand and
turned the three of
them back into fairies.
Jack Frost leaped out
of his throne with a
howl of rage.

"Who let you in?" he
bellowed. "Give me that
bracelet back and get out
of my castle!"

Maria shook her head.
Around them, the goblins had
stopped cleaning and were
messing around and squabbling.

"Now I have my bracelet back, the
goblins don't want to do nice things for
you any more," she told Jack Frost.

"You might as well give the other items back right now," added Kirsty. Jack Frost shook his fist at them. "You'll never get them back," he shouted. "I'm going to hide them for ever, in the human world."

There was a flash of blue lightning and a crack of thunder, and then Jack Frost had disappeared. Rachel, Kirsty and Maria looked at each other.

"We did it!" said Kirsty.

They all shared a big hug. The goblins were rampaging around them, getting louder and louder.

"Let's go back to my cottage," said Maria. "Do you think we can work out a way to find out where Jack Frost has gone?"

"Of course we can," said Rachel. "We will never let him win!"

The Handy
Handbag

Contents

Chapter Six: Problems with Presents   65

Chapter Seven: Flower Thieves   75

Chapter Eight: Gooey Gunge Cakes   87

Chapter Nine: Mummy Frost   97

Chapter Ten: Picnic Plans   107

Problems with Presents

Rachel and Kirsty were sitting at the round kitchen table in Maria's cottage. Maria lifted her flowery teapot and poured each of them a hot cup of tea.

"It's wonderful to have the brilliant bracelet back where it belongs," she said. "I hope that we are just as lucky with

the handy handbag and the mummy
mirror. Where do you think we should
start our search?"

"Oh no," said Rachel with a start.
"What happened to your cushion?"

The lovely unicorn cushion she had
noticed earlier was stained and frayed.

Kirsty glanced up at the painting she
had liked. It was wonky and a little torn.

"How could that have happened while
we were out?" she asked.

"It must be because of the handy
handbag," said Maria with a groan.
"Do you remember I told you that it
takes care of the gifts that children have
given their mums? I have a copy of every
present here in my cottage, so this must
be what is happening to presents in the
human world too."

Kirsty thought about the table at the youth club. It was full of presents that the children had bought for their mothers.

"If your things are getting spoiled, the presents at the youth club must be in danger, too," she said to Maria.

"You're right," said Maria, jumping to her feet. "Come on, I'll take you straight back there and we'll see if we can do anything to help."

She raised her wand and there was
a loud whooshing sound. Rachel and
Kirsty felt themselves being lifted into
the air and then they were spun around
faster than a merry-go-round. When the
spinning stopped, they were fluttering
against the ceiling of the church hall.

"It looks better than the last time we were here," said Rachel with a smile. "I'm so glad that the brilliant bracelet is safe again."

In the hall below, the children were working on the Mother's Day cards and banner.

"Oh no, look at the gift table," said Kirsty in alarm.

Rachel and Maria gasped. Ornaments, mirrors, glasses and mugs filled the table just as before, but now they looked very different. Every single one was broken or chipped. Scarves, gloves and hats were stained and dirty.

Suddenly, a little boy started to cry.

"I can't find the present I bought for my mum," he wailed.

The youth club leader, Eliza, put her

arm around him and started to help him
search.

"I can't understand why everything
seems to be going wrong today," the
fairies heard her say.

"It's falling apart," grumbled one of the
girls who was working on the banner.
"Our big surprise is going to be ruined."

Everyone in the hall was grumbling
about their projects or searching for
missing belongings.

"Where's my present for my mum?"
cried another girl. "I put it down right
here."

Kirsty tugged at Rachel's sleeve and
pointed out through the window.

"Look," she said in an urgent whisper.
"It's Jack Frost."

Sure enough, the Ice Lord was strutting

along the street outside the youth club.
Behind him was a line of goblins dressed
like children in jeans, green T-shirts and
green caps.

"Let's follow them," said Maria. "They
might lead us to the other missing
objects."

Rachel and Kirsty followed her out of
the hall. They zoomed along the street,

following Jack Frost and his train of goblins.

"Keep up!" Jack Frost barked at the goblins. "Stop dawdling, you useless pack of nincompoops. Walk at my speed. You're not snails! Do as you're told! Being a mum should be about getting presents and attention, not just telling you lot what to do."

As he strode along, he took off his
billowing cloak. Rachel, Kirsty and
Maria gasped in surprise.

"Oh my goodness, just look at him,"
said Rachel. "What is he wearing?"

Flower Thieves

Jack Frost's arms were jangling with bracelets. His neck was hidden under layers of necklaces and he was wearing three dresses, as well as two hats. He carried three handbags. Lots of of clip-on earrings were dangling from his ears. He had odd shoes and false eyelashes. He was even wearing a curly blonde wig.

"Those things do not belong to him," said Maria, folding her arms.

"His hands look bigger than usual," said Kirsty in a puzzled voice.

"I think he's wearing lots of gloves," said Rachel, peering at Jack Frost's hands. "Yes, I can see at least three different colours." Jack Frost staggered slightly, and then stopped and put his hands on his sides.

"He seems to be rather out of

breath," said Rachel.

"That's not surprising," said Maria. "All those decorations and clothes must be weighing him down. You know, I think he's wearing all the things that children have bought for their mothers. Yes, he must have the handy handbag with him. That's the only way he could have got all those things."

Kirsty and Rachel exchanged excited smiles.

"You're so clever to have worked that out," said Rachel.

"I wonder why the presents aren't broken like the ones in the hall," said Kirsty.

"It's because the handy handbag is protecting them from being spoiled or broken," said Maria.

They watched Jack Frost wobbling
down Tippington High Street. He pulled
faces at everyone he passed, and shoppers
were edging away and staring at him
over their shoulders.

Meanwhile, the goblins were running
in all directions. They were bumping into
people, crashing into shop displays and
making a terrible hullabaloo. Dogs were
barking and howling at them, and some

of the goblins were barking back.

"Goblins certainly love to make a nuisance of themselves," said Maria with a sigh.

The fairies hovered above the heads of the other shoppers, listening to what they were saying.

"What rude children," said one lady, tutting to her friend.

Three goblins pushed past her, squawking with laughter.

"Their mother should be stopping them," said a man, glaring at Jack Frost.

Jack Frost glared back and stuck out his tongue.

"Those boys made me drop my shopping," cried a young woman.

"You should keep your children under

control," an elderly man told Jack Frost.

"Mind your own business," said Jack Frost, grinning.

"Why does he look so happy?" asked Maria.

"Because he loves being the centre of attention," said Kirsty. "Everyone is looking at him and talking about him. It's Jack Frost's idea of the best day ever."

Just then, Jack Frost darted across the street and squashed his nose against the window of a florist's shop. There was a poster in the window with a picture of a boy giving his mother a

big bunch of flowers.

He whirled around with a deep roar of outrage.

"Mothers get flowers!" he blasted out. "I don't just want presents, you gormless green nitwits. If I have to be a mother to you lot, I want flowers!"

The goblins jumped as if they had
been stung. Then they raced towards a
raised flowerbed in the middle of the
street, where a little wooden sign said
'Remember to visit the Tippington
Bakery'.

"We have to stop them," cried Kirsty.

But the goblins were already yanking
up handfuls of flowers by the roots and
hurling them at Jack Frost.

"Stop that, you naughty boys!" the
young woman called out.

"Those flowers belong to everyone,"
the elderly man exclaimed. "You're not
allowed to pick them."

Rachel had tears in her eyes.

"They're spoiling Tippington," she cried. "They're ruining my lovely home town!"

Gooey Gunge Cakes

The three fairies fluttered down and perched on a lamppost.

"We can't let the goblins cause any more damage," said Maria in a firm voice. "We have to get them away from Tippington as fast as we can. I'll send them to Fairyland."

She raised her wand, but Rachel stopped her.

"You can't use magic," said Rachel. "All the shoppers are staring at Jack Frost and the goblins."

"I've got an idea," said Kirsty. "We need a way to lead the goblins away from the high street. If we can find a quiet spot, Maria could use her magic without being seen."

"That's a great idea, Kirsty," said Maria. "And I know the perfect thing to lure the goblins away. Keep your eyes on the bakery sign."

She winked at Rachel and Kirsty and then waved her wand. Instantly, the words on the sign swirled around and changed. It now said 'FREE gooey gunge cakes THIS WAY'. An arrow pointed down a

FREE gooey gunge cakes THIS WAY

narrow alleyway.

As soon as the goblins noticed the sign, they squealed in excitement and scrambled off the raised flowerbed. Within seconds, they had all disappeared down the alleyway. Rachel breathed a sigh of relief, and Kirsty laughed.

"Only goblins could be interested in an offer like that," she said. "I don't think any humans are likely to follow them!"

Jack Frost had turned back to stare at the florist shop's poster of a mother getting flowers from her son.

"I'm starting to think that mums have no fun," he muttered.

He hadn't realised that all the goblins had disappeared.

"Let's go," said Rachel. "As soon as they are back in Fairyland, we can go back and try to get the handy handbag from Jack Frost."

She zoomed off down the alleyway, followed by Kirsty and Maria. As they went, Maria flicked her wand back over her shoulder and returned the bakery sign to its normal wording.

The goblins were down at the end of
the alleyway, searching everywhere for
the free gunge cakes. The fairies stopped
in mid-air and hovered in front of them.

"Thank goodness we got them away
from town," said Kirsty. "But we're no
closer to getting the handy handbag
back."

"Fairies!" shrieked the tallest goblin,
pointing his finger at them. "You've

tricked us, you meanies."

"Where are all the gunge cakes?"
wailed the goblin next to him. "Have you
eaten them all?"

"I don't think there *are* any gunge
cakes," said a third goblin with a scowl.
"The fairies lied to
us."

"I would never tell
a lie," said Maria in
a cool, clear voice.
"Please hold out
your hands."

She waved her
wand and each
goblin found a green
cake in his hands.
They all shoved
the strange-looking

cakes into their mouths.

"He's got a bigger cake than me," said the tallest goblin, pointing at another goblin. "Not fair!"

The goblins immediately started yelling at each other and arguing about who had the biggest cake. Crumbs sprayed everywhere.

"I'd better send them home before they run off again," said Maria.

She raised her wand and the goblins disappeared in a puff of green sparkles.

"They're safely back in the goblin village," Maria said.

"Yes!" said Kirsty, high-fiving Rachel.
"Now we can concentrate on following
Jack Frost and getting the handy
handbag back. Quick, let's hurry back to
the high street."

When they returned, the high street
looked quite normal again. Jack Frost
had disappeared, and the shoppers were
once more bustling along the street.

"He might still be somewhere nearby,"
said Kirsty.

"He should be easy to spot in his
strange outfit," said Rachel. "Time for a
game of hide-and-seek!"

Mummy Frost

The fairies fluttered along the high street, flying as low as they dared. They peered into shop after shop, looking for a flash of golden necklaces or a swish of curly blonde hair. But they reached the end of the high street without seeing Jack Frost.

"He isn't in the shops," said Maria. "Maybe he's gone back to Fairyland."

"No, he hasn't," said Rachel suddenly.

She pointed at a post box on the corner. Sticking out from behind it was a pair of large feet. One was wearing a white high-heeled shoe, and the other was wearing a flowery welly boot.

Putting her finger to her lips, Kirsty led Rachel and Maria over to flutter above the post box. They looked down and saw Jack Frost hunched over with his bottom sticking up in the air. His bags were scattered around him.

"What's he doing?" asked Rachel in a puzzled voice.

"He's saying something," said Maria. "Let's listen."

"Stupid, pesky goblins," Jack Frost was muttering crossly to himself. "I've had enough of being a mum. I thought it would be fun, but they just follow me around and squawk at me. They never do as they're told. All they do is pester, pester, pester all day long. That's not the right kind of attention."

"He's hiding from

the goblins!" said Kirsty.

Maria gave a sudden squeak of excitement.

"Look at his handbags," she said. "Do you see that peach-coloured one in front of him with the bow on it? That's my handy handbag!"

Kirsty clapped her hands together and Rachel hugged Maria.

"I've got an idea," she said. "Jack Frost is hiding because he doesn't like being needed and followed around. Maybe Kirsty and I should become goblins again. He might forget

all about his bags if he's trying to get
away from us."

"That's a fantastic idea, Rachel," said
Maria. "Look, there's a telephone box
over there. Let's hide behind it so I can do
some magic."

The three fairies fluttered down behind

the telephone
box and Maria
tapped each
of the girls
with her wand.
Instantly they
felt themselves
growing
bigger. Their
feet became
enormous and
their knees

and elbows grew knobbly. Their hair disappeared and their noses grew long and hooked. POP! POP! POP! Warts sprang up all over their faces.

"Mummy!" squealed Rachel. "I need a cuddle!"

"Mummy! Mummy!" squawked Kirsty. "I need a nose-blow!"

They pelted towards Jack Frost, and he turned around looking horrified.

"Leave me alone!" he roared. "I don't want to be a mummy any more. It's too much hard work!"

He gathered up his handbags and ran. Rachel and Kirsty followed him as fast as they could, calling out everything that might need a mummy's help.

"I need a wee!"

"My legs hurt!"

"I want a snack!"

"I'm bored!"

"I want to go home!"

Jack Frost sprinted down an alleyway. His wig flew off and one of his necklaces broke. Beads scattered

behind him and the girls leaped over them.

"Are we nearly there yet?" called Kirsty.

Jack Frost looked back over his shoulder in alarm, and at that moment he tripped over the hem of one of his dresses. CRASH! He sprawled on to the ground, and bags, gloves, hats, scarves, bracelets

and necklaces flew into the air. Rachel and Kirsty skidded to a halt.

"Catch!" cried Rachel.

Picnic Plans

The sparkling handy handbag landed in
Kirsty's outstretched goblin arms. Smiling,
she looked up and saw Maria fluttering
towards her. As soon as the little fairy
touched the bag, it shrank to its proper
size. Maria hooked it over her arm and
waved her wand. In a flash, Rachel and

Kirsty were human girls again. At the same moment, all the things that Jack Frost had stolen suddenly disappeared.

"You three rotten ratbags!" said Jack Frost, scrambling to his feet. "Give me back my things."

"They're not yours," said Maria. "I have returned them to their rightful owners, ready for Mother's Day. And all the gifts that were ruined when you stole the handbag will be as good as new."

Jack Frost scowled.

"I'm fed up with you fairies," he snarled. "You're always trying to steal my limelight. One way or another, there's only going to be one star of Mother's Day this year. Me!"

He stuck his tongue out at them and disappeared in a

flash of blue lightning.

"Thank goodness," said Rachel, turning to Maria with a smile. "We did it!"

"Thank you both with all my heart," said Maria. "I couldn't have got my handbag back without you. It's time for me to take it back to Fairyland, but

I'll be back as soon as I have any news about the mummy mirror."

"We'll see you soon," said Kirsty.

There was a sparkling puff of fairy dust, and Maria disappeared. Holding hands, Rachel and Kirsty headed back towards the church hall.

"The flowerbed is back to normal," said Kirsty, smiling. "Maria must have used her magic to repair the flowers."

As they passed a gift shop, Rachel spotted a rose-pink fan in the window.

"Mum would love that," she said.

She bought it and then the girls hurried to the church hall. It was bustling with activity. All the presents were as good as new and being wrapped at the table. The cards were almost finished and Eliza had a team of children working on the picnic plans. She smiled when she saw Rachel and Kirsty.

"Everything is going well," she said.

"Each person is going to bring one thing to the picnic tomorrow. That way there is sure to be enough food. Do you want to sign up?"

"Sure," said Kirsty. "I'll bring a bowl of strawberries."

"And I'll bring a pot of cream," Rachel promised.

While Kirsty signed them up for the

picnic, Rachel went over to the table to wrap her mum's present and make a card. The hall was filled with excited chatter. Everyone was looking forward to the picnic.

"It's going to be perfect," said Kirsty. "Just as long we can find the mummy mirror before tomorrow!"

The Mummy
Mirror

Contents

Chapter Eleven: Maria in Danger   121

Chapter Twelve: Rachel and
Kirsty to the Rescue   129

Chapter Thirteen: Jack Frost's Triumph   141

Chapter Fourteen: No Magic   151

Chapter Fifteen: The Best
Mother's Day Ever   161

Maria in Danger

"It's Mother's Day!" said Kirsty, sitting bolt upright in bed. "What time is the picnic?"

It was Sunday morning. Shafts of spring sunshine were darting through the curtains, and Rachel's bedroom was full of light. Rachel sat up and looked over at Kirsty. "The picnic's at lunchtime," she said. "But we've got a lot to do before then."

She jumped out of bed, flung her window wide open and breathed in the scent of flowers and fresh air.

"It's the perfect day for a picnic," she went on. "As long as we can get the mummy mirror back from Jack Frost."

"We can do it," said Kirsty. "Yesterday

we found two missing objects, and now there's only one left to find."

The girls hurried to get dressed and brush their hair. Rachel was looking forward to running into her mum's room to wish her a happy Mother's Day. But just as she was about to go, a soft breeze puffed her curtains into her room. Something small came flying in with the breeze and tumbled across Kirsty's bed.

"It's Maria!" Kirsty exclaimed.

The girls kneeled beside the bed and gazed in concern at the tiny fairy. Her hair was tangled by the wind and she had a confused expression on her face.

Maria sat up, smoothed down her ruffled hair and fluttered her wings. Then she noticed the girls, and stared at them with a puzzled frown.

"Who are you?" she asked. "And where am I?"

Her voice sounded different. It was sing-song and faraway. Rachel and Kirsty exchanged a worried look.

"You're at my house," said Rachel. "I'm Rachel and this is Kirsty. We've been helping you get your things back from Jack Frost, remember?"

"Have you come straight from Fairyland?" asked Kirsty.

"Fairyland?" repeated Maria in a surprised voice.

She said it as if she had never heard the word before.

"Yes, Fairyland," Rachel repeated. "With the Seeing Pool and the palace, and toadstool houses ..."

Maria gave her head a little shake. When she spoke again, her voice sounded like normal. "Of course," she said. "Sorry, I don't know what came over me then."

"You look a bit pale," said Kirsty. "Are you feeling OK?"

Maria fluttered over to Rachel's dressing table and looked at herself in the mirror. Then she turned to the girls with a shocked expression.

"I'm not just pale," she said. "I'm almost

see-through. Girls, I think I'm fading away! This must be happening because my mummy mirror is missing," finished Maria.

She turned and looked at the girls, her eyes brimming with tears.

"Why is the mummy mirror making you fade away?" asked Kirsty.

"It helps me to remember my special job, and how to help all the mothers I've ever met," Maria explained. "Without it, I'm going to start to forget things. Eventually I'll even forget myself. And then I'll just fade away to nothing!"

Rachel and Kirsty
to the Rescue

Kirsty and Rachel looked at each other
in horror.

"I knew the Mother's Day picnic was
in danger," said Rachel. "But the idea of
Maria fading away is even worse!"

"We can't let that happen," said Kirsty

with determination. "We have to find the
mummy mirror before it's too late."

Maria sat down on Rachel's jewellery
box, and the girls noticed that her eyes
looked misty and distant.

"What day is it today?" she asked in a
dreamy voice.

"It's Mother's Day," said Rachel.
"Maria, you have to remember."

"Mother's Day," Maria repeated. "The magic of motherhood."

"Yes," said Kirsty. "That's right – it's your magic that helps to make the day so special."

"Which day?" Maria asked.

Rachel and Kirsty looked at each other and groaned.

"We have to find Jack Frost and his goblins," said Rachel. "If we can't get the mummy mirror back, Mother's Day will be ruined and Maria will disappear for ever."

"But how are we going to find them without Maria?" Kirsty asked. "While she's like this, she won't be able to help us. I don't think she'll even be able to remember us."

Maria yawned and blinked. She was

growing paler than ever.

"Maybe you should go back to
Fairyland," said Rachel.

"That sounds nice," said Maria,
yawning again. "How do I get there? Do
I need a ticket?"

"Oh my goodness," said Kirsty. "This
is terrible. I don't think she even knows
that she can do magic. We have to find
somewhere safe for her to stay while we

try to put things right."

"I think I know the perfect place," said
Rachel.

She reached under her bed and pulled
out her craft box. From a brown paper
bag, she pulled out a few small squares of
material and a handful of cotton-wool
balls.

"I got these samples
from the fabric
shop," she
explained.

Next, Rachel
opened the
front of her
dolls' house.
All her dolls
were lying in
their wooden beds.

She took her best doll out of the largest bedroom and used the fabric squares and cotton wool to make the bed soft and warm.

"Come and rest in this bed, Maria," she said. "No one will disturb you here."

"How can I get all the way over there?" Maria asked.

She had forgotten that she could fly. Feeling very sorry for the confused little fairy, Kirsty laid her hand flat on the dressing table, palm up.

"Step on to my hand and I'll carry you there," she said.

She lifted Maria over to the dolls' house and carefully tucked her into the bed.

"Get some sleep," said Rachel. "Kirsty and I will find a way to put everything right. We won't let you fade away."

"Thank you," Maria whispered.

She closed her eyes and the girls shut the front of the dolls' house. Then Kirsty looked at her best friend, feeling worried.

"What are we going to do now?" she asked.

"We have to get to Fairyland without Maria's help," said Rachel. "I'm sure that's where we'll find Jack Frost. And I only know one way to get there without a fairy wand."

"Of course!" Kirsty exclaimed.

She and Rachel felt for the chains around their necks and pulled out their matching lockets. During their first adventures with the fairies, Queen Titania had given them the lockets to say thank you for their help. Inside, there was just enough sparkling fairy dust for a trip to Fairyland.

The girls opened their lockets.

"Shall we go to the Fairyland Palace?" asked Rachel.

Kirsty shook her head.

"I think we have to go straight to Jack Frost's castle," she said.

Rachel gasped.

"But we won't have any magic to protect us," she said.

"I know," said Kirsty. "But what if we get to the palace and find that the king and queen are away? Or worse still, what if Jack Frost has used Maria's magic to harm the palace? He's done it before. I think we have to rely on each other. I know we can defeat Jack Frost if we work as a team, even without magic."

Smiling at each other, the best friends sprinkled their fairy dust over themselves and held hands.

"Take us to Jack Frost's castle," they said in unison.

Jack Frost's Triumph

At once, the fairy dust whooshed
around them, wrapping them up in a
safe, sparkly cocoon of magic. They felt
themselves shrinking to fairy size, while
gauzy wings fluttered on their backs.
Rachel's bedroom became blurry and
the colours faded. It was replaced by a

dazzling whiteness and a biting wind. The girls blinked.

"We're flying towards Jack Frost's castle," said Kirsty. "We did it, Rachel! We're here."

Below, everything was covered in a deep layer of snow. The sky was a mass of thick, grey clouds, and the Ice Castle looked colder than ever.

"I can't see any goblins guarding the battlements," said Rachel. "Let's see if we can get in through the trapdoor."

In the past, they had sometimes been able to creep into the castle through the hidden trapdoor in the battlements. Keeping their fingers crossed that no goblin guards would suddenly appear, Rachel and Kirsty fluttered up to the top of the castle. They quickly saw the trapdoor, which was set into the floor. It was a slab of solid ice, with a metal ring in the top.

"I wish we had fairy magic to open it up," Kirsty whispered.

"Me too," said Rachel with a smile. "But we're just going to have to pull."

The trapdoor was incredibly heavy and the cold metal froze their hands, but they couldn't give up. Heaving and straining, they managed to lift the icy slab. Inside, they saw the winding ice steps that led to the ground floor of the castle.

Silently, the best friends flew down the steps. But as they went deeper, they heard a loud bang above their heads. They stopped and looked up. It seemed darker.

"What was that?" Kirsty asked.

Suddenly, three goblins leaped around the corner and flung a net over their heads. They were knocked to the ground, and the goblins squawked with laughter.

"That was the sound of the trapdoor slamming shut," said the tallest goblin, giving them a mean smile. "You're our prisoners now!"

Rachel and Kirsty were trapped. With their arms, legs and wings tangled in the net, they were dragged along corridors and down steps until they reached the Throne Room. There, Jack Frost was sitting on his throne. He pointed at them and cackled with laughter.

"You girls are my prisoners now," he told them. "Look up and say hello to your new home."

Two cages were dangling from the ceiling of the Throne Room. Jack Frost waved his wand, and Rachel and Kirsty were suddenly inside the cages.

"Let us go," said Rachel. "You can't keep us here."

"No whingeing allowed," Jack Frost snapped. "I *can* keep you here, and I am going to keep you here. There's nothing you can do about it."

He held up a mirror and waved it at the girls.

"Take a good look at yourselves," he said. "Now you can see what happens to pesky fairies who try to stop my fun."

The mirror was golden with a pink heart picture on the lid. It had a certain glow about it that the girls recognised at once.

"That's not yours," said Kirsty. "That's Maria's mummy mirror."

"Wrong," Jack Frost snapped. "It's mine now. Mine, mine, mine. I've won!"

No Magic

Rachel and Kirsty put their arms through
the bars of their cages and reached out to
one another. Their fingers laced together.

"Don't worry, we'll think of something,"
said Rachel. "As long as we have each
other, there is always hope."

The best friends watched as the goblins
ran around the Throne Room, waiting

on Jack Frost and squabbling with each other. The Ice Lord himself stayed on his throne, holding the mummy mirror.

At first, he kept looking into the mirror. But after a while he shook it and stamped his foot.

"Where has my reflection gone?" he demanded. "Who are all these humans? I don't want to look at humans."

The goblins didn't answer him. Next, he held the mirror to his ear.

"Now it's talking to me," he grumbled. "I don't want to know what mummies are doing in the human world." He shook the mirror again and then frowned at it. "Stop telling me about nappies and kisses and talcum powder. Shut up!"

Rachel and Kirsty watched as Jack Frost carried on yelling at the mirror. Then he buried it under his throne cushions.

"It looks as if the mummy mirror isn't what he expected," said Rachel. "I wonder if there's any way we can use this to get free."

"I can still hear it!" Jack Frost yelled.

He picked up two more throne cushions and put them on either side of his head

like earmuffs. He didn't notice one of the goblins pick up the mummy mirror and open it.

"Ooh, look, that mummy's baking," he said. The other goblins crowded around, making hungry noises and rubbing their bellies. Jack Frost spotted what they were doing and snatched the mummy mirror back.

"Get back to work," he barked at the goblins. "Clear off!"

He flung himself back on his throne, his

mouth turning downwards at the corners.

"All I ever wanted was to be the star of Mother's Day," he said, folding his arms. "Why should I have to listen to all these silly human mothers?"

"'The star of Mother's Day'," Kirsty repeated. "Rachel, this gives me an idea."

Kirsty rattled the bars of her cage and shouted down to Jack Frost.

"Hey," she said. "If you give back Maria's mirror and send us back to the human world, you can be a star, just like you want."

"What are you blithering on about?" Jack Frost demanded. "How can you make me a star?"

"All you have to do is give back the mirror and return us to the human world," Kirsty replied. "Then you can be the star of the Mother's Day picnic – as Frosty and the Gobolicious Band. I bet that the children and their mums would love to have live music at the celebration."

Jack Frost narrowed his eyes.

"You can't trick me," he hissed, curling his fingers tightly around the mirror. "I'm not giving this mirror back. It's mine!"

"Oh, OK," said Kirsty, shrugging. "I guess you'll just have to keep it under your cushions so it's not so noisy. Will you sleep with it under your pillow at night?"

"It's a shame that he won't have the fun of performing at an important picnic," said Rachel in a loud voice.

"I know, but it's his choice," said Kirsty, shrugging again.

There was silence for a moment, and then the mirror started to make noise again. Jack Frost gritted his teeth and then uncurled his fingers. The mirror gleamed in the palm of his hand.

"Fine," he said in a grumpy voice.

"Take the mirror. But you had better keep your side of the bargain and let me perform."

Rachel and Kirsty smiled at each other.

"We promise," they said together.

CRACK! Jack Frost waved his wand and ice-blue lightning bolts flashed around them.

The Best Mother's Day Ever

Rachel and Kirsty covered their eyes as the lightning crackled. Then everything went quiet. They looked up and saw that they were back in Rachel's bedroom, and they were human again. Kirsty was holding the mummy mirror in her hand.

"Quickly!" said Rachel.

They rushed to the dolls' house. Maria
was lying where they had left her.
She was so pale that she was almost
transparent. With gentle hands, Rachel
lifted the bed out of the dolls' house.
Kirsty touched the mirror to the little
fairy's hand.

Then everything happened very fast.
The mirror shrank to fairy size, while
Maria's colour came rushing back. Her
eyes sparkled and she darted out of the
bed. The little fabric squares fluttered to
the floor.

"How did you
do it?" she cried,
examining herself
in amazement.

Rachel and
Kirsty felt their
cheeks burning.

"We couldn't let
you fade away,"
said Rachel.

"You have
saved the magic
of motherhood,"

Maria told them. "Thank you from the bottom of my heart. I'll never forget how you have helped me."

She tapped her wand on their lockets, which filled up with fairy dust again. Then, with a final wave, she disappeared back to Fairyland.

Rachel and Kirsty shared a happy hug, and then Rachel checked her watch.

"It's time to go and tell my mum about the picnic," she said. "I think this is going to be a lot of fun!"

A short time later, Rachel and Kirsty were sitting on a large picnic rug with Mrs Walker. In the middle of the rug were bowls and plates piled high with sandwiches, fruit, pasties, dips, salads

and cupcakes. All around the rug, happy mothers were sharing the celebration with their children. Cards, presents and ripped wrapping paper surrounded each family group.

"Are you having a happy Mother's Day?" Rachel asked her mum.

"It's the best one ever," said Mrs Walker with a smile.

"I'm looking forward to seeing my mum later," said Kirsty.

A little girl nearby looked at Kirsty with sad eyes.

"My mum can't be here today," she said. "I miss her."

"Poor girl," whispered Kirsty to Rachel. "I wish we could do something to help her,"

Just then, the surface of the pond

nearby started to sparkle.

"That's not the sparkle of sunshine on water," said Rachel in surprise. "That's magic."

The water shimmered, and then the girls saw Maria's face smiling at them through the ripples.

"I'm speaking to you through the Seeing Pool at the Fairyland Palace," she said, her voice like a distant echo. "Don't

worry about the little girl. That's what I'm here for. The magic of mums is all around, whether they're near or far – thanks to you."

Behind her, the kind face of Queen Titania appeared, smiling. Rachel and Kirsty looked over to where the girl was sitting, and saw that she was already laughing and smiling, just as if her mum were there beside her.

"Maria's magic really is the best Mother's Day gift ever," said Kirsty.

When they glanced back at the water, Maria and the queen had disappeared. The pond was just an ordinary pond again.

Suddenly there was the twanging, clanging, jangling sound of instruments being tuned. The girls whirled around and saw that a small stage had appeared under the trees. Frosty and the Gobolicious Band looked happy and excited, and everyone at the picnic was smiling.

"Let's go and start the dancing," said Rachel, grinning at her best friend. "I think this is going to be Jack Frost's best Mother's Day ever too!"

The End

Rae the
Rollercoaster Fairy

Read on for a sneak peek…

Rachel Walker cartwheeled her way
along the pavement towards her school.
She was excited that her best friend
Kirsty Tate had come to stay with her.
They were on their way to a summer
funfair on the playing field at Rachel's
school.

"Watch out for the lamppost," called
Kirsty from behind her.

Giggling and panting, Rachel jumped
up. She had felt fizzy with fun ever
since she had woken up. Today was the

opening morning of the funfair, and they had agreed to get there early so that they could enjoy it for as long as possible.

"This is going to be so much fun," Rachel said. "I just know it."

"Me too," said Kirsty. "But we always have fun together."

"Especially when we're on a fairy adventure," Rachel added, lowering her voice in case anyone was listening.

Since the girls first met on Rainspell Island, they had shared many magical adventures. Their friendship with the fairies was a secret that they had promised to keep for ever.

"Oh my goodness, look," said Rachel, pointing at the trees ahead.

The top of a Ferris wheel was poking up above the branches.

"And look behind it," said Kirsty,

jumping up and down on the spot.
"Rachel, it's a rollercoaster!"

Sure enough, a silvery rollercoaster
track was arching and dipping on the
other side of the Ferris wheel. Rachel felt
a thrilling tingle run through her body.
She looked at Kirsty, knowing that her
best friend was bubbling with the same
excitement.

"Let's run," she said. "Let's get there as
fast as we can."

Giggling, the best friends sprinted along
the pavement, all the time glimpsing
more and more of the funfair through
the trees ahead. Breathlessly, they called
out to each other every time they saw
something new.

"Candyfloss!"

"Dodgems!"

"Helter-skelter!"

Large signs pointed the way towards the entrance, and at last they arrived, their hearts racing. An arched gateway had been set up at the end of the school playing field, and the sign above it was printed in bright, bold lettering: *The Fernandos' Fabulous Funfair*.

Read **Rae the Rollercoaster Fairy** to find out what adventures are in store for Kirsty and Rachel!

Calling all parents, carers and teachers!
The Rainbow Magic fairies are here to help
your child enter the magical world of reading.
Whatever reading stage they are at, there's
a Rainbow Magic book for everyone!
Here is Lydia the Reading Fairy's guide to
supporting your child's journey at all levels.

Starting Out

Our Rainbow Magic Beginner Readers are perfect for first-time readers who are just beginning to develop reading skills and confidence. Approved by teachers, they contain a full range of educational levelling, as well as lively full-colour illustrations.

Developing Readers

Rainbow Magic Early Readers contain longer stories and wider vocabulary for building stamina and growing confidence. These are adaptations of our most popular Rainbow Magic stories, specially developed for younger readers in conjunction with an Early Years reading consultant, with full-colour illustrations.

Going Solo

The Rainbow Magic chapter books – a mixture of series and one-off specials – contain accessible writing to encourage your child to venture into reading independently. These highly collectible and much-loved magical stories inspire a love of reading to last a lifetime.

www.rainbowmagicbooks.co.uk

"Rainbow Magic got my daughter reading chapter books. Great sparkly covers, cute fairies and traditional stories full of magic that she found impossible to put down" - Mother of Edie (6 years)

"Florence LOVES the Rainbow Magic books. She really enjoys reading now" - Mother of Florence (6 years)

The Rainbow Magic Reading Challenge

Well done, fairy friend – you have completed the book!
This book was worth 10 points.

See how far you have climbed on the
Reading Rainbow opposite.

The more books you read, the more points you will get,
and the closer you will be to becoming a Fairy Princess!

Do you want your own Reading Rainbow?
1. Cut out the coin below
2. Go to the Rainbow Magic website
3. Download and print out your poster
4. Add your coin and climb up the Reading Rainbow!

There's all this and lots more at
www.rainbowmagicbooks.co.uk

You'll find activities, competitions, stories, a special
newsletter and complete profiles of all the
Rainbow Magic fairies. Find a fairy with your name!